Dewey Doo-it™
Feeds a Friend

By Brahm Wenger & Alan Green   Illustrated by Jean Gillmore

For Lori, Laurel and Pam

Special thanks to: Marcia Leonard, Ken Leonard, Aurora Winter and Roy Clark

Library of Congress Control Number: 2003097167

Dewey Doo-it is a registered trademark of The Helpful Doo-its Project LLC.
Published by RandallFraser Publishing
2082 Business Center Drive, Suite 163
Irvine, CA 92612

Here's Dewey Doo-it!

Dewey lives in the Jingle Jangle Jungle with his older brother Howie Doo-it and his little sister Anita Doo-it.

Sometimes Howie wants to play with Dewey.

Sometimes Anita wants to play with Dewey.

And sometimes they *both* want to play with Dewey at the same time!

One hot summer day, Dewey made a new friend—a turtle named Marty.

Dewey invited Marty to play ring-toss in the park with Howie and
Anita. Soon they were joined by their friends Kenya Doo-it and the twins,
Woody Doo-it and Willie Doo-it. "Let's make a big circle," Dewey said,
handing out the rings. "Who wants to be the first catcher?"

"I do, I do," said Marty, stretching out his long, long neck. "Let 'em fly!"
The Doo-its threw their rings high into the air. Up, up, up they went. Red. Blue.
Orange. Green. Marty was fast. He darted around the circle catching all the rings.
The Doo-its played ring-toss with Marty every day that summer.

But one day Marty didn't come to play.

"Where is he?" asked Dewey. "He's never been late for ring-toss before."

"I wonder what's keeping him," said Howie.

"I'm sure he'll show up soon," said Kenya.

But he never did.

Dewey was worried. He decided to go look for Marty.

"He's not here!" he said, looking in the pond where they first met.

"He's not here either," he said, searching inside their secret cave.

Where was Marty? Determined to find him, Dewey hiked up the big hill to the place where Marty lived.

Marty looked very sad.
"What's wrong?" Dewey asked. "Don't you like playing ring-toss anymore?"
"I can't play," Marty sighed. "I'm too tired."

"Tired?" Dewey was confused. "Maybe you should take a nap."

"No!" Marty cried, "I don't need a nap. I need food! I haven't had anything to eat for days. I'm tired because I'm hungry!"

Dewey was shocked. He looked up at Marty's tree. "What happened to all your food?" he asked.

"A big wind came swooping out of
the night sky and blew away all my
fruit!" Marty explained.
"Everything's gone now."
  Marty was in trouble.
But Dewey had an idea.

He ran back down to the park where there was a big fruit tree with lots of juicy pears and apples and oranges. But no matter how hard he tried, no matter how high he jumped, Dewey Doo-it couldn't do it. He was just too small. "How will I ever get the fruit down from the tree?"

Dewey thought,

and thought,

and thought some more.

But still, *Dewey Doo-it couldn't do it.*

Just then Howie and Anita came by. Dewey told them, "Marty is getting weaker and weaker every minute. We need to get food for him right away!"

Howie pointed up at the big fruit tree and stated the obvious, "You need to get the fruit down from those branches up there," he declared.

"I know *that*," Dewey replied. "But tell me...*how we do it, Howie Doo-it!*"

Before Howie could answer they spotted a group of ants carrying a freshly plucked leaf from the tree.

"Look at that!" Dewey said. "Those tiny ants have given me a wonderful idea. We need teamwork! Our friends can help us climb up to get the fruit down from the tree—just like those ants."

The tree was very tall and the Doo-its were very small, but that didn't bother them at all. They stood on each other's shoulders and made a food chain to pass the big, juicy pears and apples and oranges to the ground. Dewey then hurried off to his house.

"We need to get much more food for Marty!" he called out. "Go pick some vegetables from the garden. I'll meet you there."

Two by two, the Doo-its carried away giant zucchinis and cucumbers and carrots and loaded them into the wagon.

Just as they finished, Dewey arrived with a big white box. He balanced it on top of the vegetables, and the helpful Doo-its started up the big hill.

Poor Marty! While the Doo-its were gathering the food, his neck had gotten shorter and shorter. Now only his little head was poking out of his shell. He was very weak.

The hill was so steep that the juicy fruits and giant vegetables kept falling off the back of the wagon. Soon everyone was exhausted.

"The wagon is so heavy!" Woody said. "I'm too tired to push anymore."

"Let's stop," Kenya said. "I need to rest."

"NO!" called Dewey. "We can't stop now, Marty's very weak. He's waiting for us to save him!" He turned to Kenya and assured her, "You can do it, Kenya Doo-it!"

Finally, the helpful Doo-its made it to the top of the hill.
"Shhhh!" Dewey whispered. "Look, Marty's sleeping. Let's set up the food and surprise him."

Quietly, they placed the fruits and vegetables on a big picnic blanket.
There were lots left over, so Kenya and the twins stored them in a hollow log.
"That should last him till his tree grows more fruit," they declared.

"Now I think it's time for a certain turtle to wake up," Dewey said. He turned to the other Doo-its. "Okay, one...two...three..." "SURPRISE!" they all shouted. But Marty didn't move.

They tried again. "One...two...three...SURPRISE!" But Marty still didn't move. Were they too late?

Dewey had an idea. He bent over and whispered in Marty's ear, "Who wants to play ring-toss?"

Marty's eye popped open. "Ring-toss?" Then he caught sight of all the food. "Oh, wow!" he said. "Look what you brought me!"

Hurray! *Dewey Doo-it finally did it!*
Marty happily munched on all the mangos, melons and tomatoes.
"We have one more treat for you," Dewey said, "and I bet you'll never guess
what it is." He opened the big white box.

"IT'S A RING-TOSS CAKE!" everyone cheered. Dewey Doo-it and the other helpful Doo-its couldn't wait to play ring-toss again. But for now they were all just happy to gather round and have a big slice of ring-toss cake...and party with Marty.

Hi Everyone!

Wasn't that a wonderful story? I loved helping my friend Marty when he had no food! This story was inspired by another person who helps people who have no food. Her name is Bea Gaddy.

When Bea didn't have enough food to feed her family, she wheeled a big garbage can around to some small grocery stores in her neighborhood to collect the food they were going to throw away. Soon her garbage can was full with enough food for her own family and her neighbors too.

Bea felt great about helping her neighbors, and soon she found other helpful Doo-its to help her. Just like the food chain we formed to get the food down from the tree, she formed a chain of helpers to give food, clothing, and even shelter to others. Now she has so many helpers that every year she serves Thanksgiving dinner to over 45,000 people.

You can be a helpful Doo-it too, just like Bea Gaddy and me!

Thanks, Dewey

D1467728

Fire

Andrew Charman

RSVP ®

RAINTREE
STECK-VAUGHN
PUBLISHERS

The Steck-Vaughn Company

Austin, Texas

Series Editor: Pippa Pollard
Editors: Clair Llewellyn and
   Kim Merlino
Design: Shaun Barlow
Project Manager and Electronic
   Production: Julie Klaus
Artwork: Ian Thompson
Cover artwork: Ian Thompson
Picture Research:
   Ambreen Husain
Educational Advisor:
   Joy Richardson

Library of Congress
Cataloging-in-Publication Data
Charman, Andrew.
   Fire / Andrew Charman.
      p.   cm. — (First starts)
   Includes index.
   Summary: Describes uses of fire, fire at the Earth's core, volcanoes, the nature of fire, making fire, and energy from fire.
   ISBN 0-8114-5511-4
   1. Fire — Juvenile literature.
[1. Fire.]   I. Title.   II. Series.
TP265.C47 1994
541.3'6—dc20   93-20873
                    CIP
                    AC

Printed and bound in the United States by Lake Book, Melrose Park, IL

1 2 3 4 5 6 7 8 9 0 LB 98 97 96 95 94 93

Contents

Fire for Life

Planet Earth is only fit for life because it is warmed by the sun. The sun is a huge, hot glowing ball. Without its heat, the Earth would be too cold for us to survive.

On Earth we use fire for many things. We use it to make things and to cook. Fire also gives us energy for heating our homes and for **transportation**.

▽ Very hot objects produce light. This is why the sun is so bright. Never look directly at the sun. You might injure your eyes.

Fire in the Earth

Deep down in the center, or core, of the Earth it is very hot - about 8,000 degrees Fahrenheit (4,500° C). The rocks of the outer core are not very deep, but they are still so hot that they are **molten**, or liquid. Above this is the mantle. Water that is heated deep in the Earth sometimes shoots to the surface in spouts, called geysers.

▷ The water in a hot spring is heated deep inside the Earth. When this water boils over, it is thrust out like a geyser.

▽ Imagine that you could take a sample of the Earth from the crust to the core. You would be able to see the different layers. The deeper you go into the Earth, the hotter it gets.

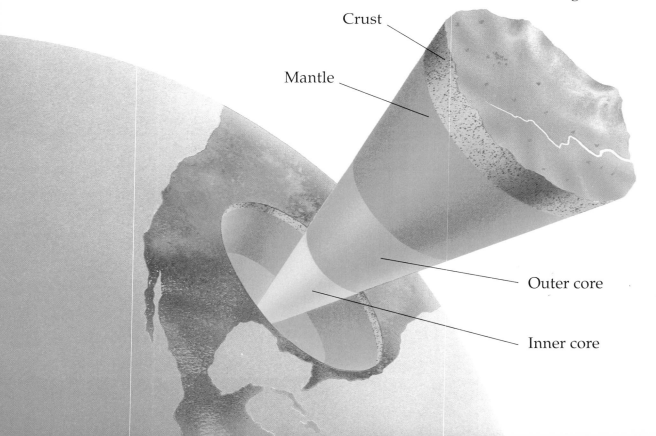

Crust

Mantle

Outer core

Inner core

▽ These monkeys are called Japanese macaques. They are keeping themselves warm by bathing in a hot spring.

Volcanoes

The molten rock deep down in the Earth is called **magma**. Volcanoes are openings in the hard surface, or **crust**, of the Earth, through which magma and gases sometimes escape. This is called an eruption. When magma reaches the surface of the Earth, it is called **lava**. When lava cools, it hardens into rock.

▽ An erupting volcano may hurl lava, smoke, and pieces of rock high into the air. It may destroy buildings and cars in nearby towns.

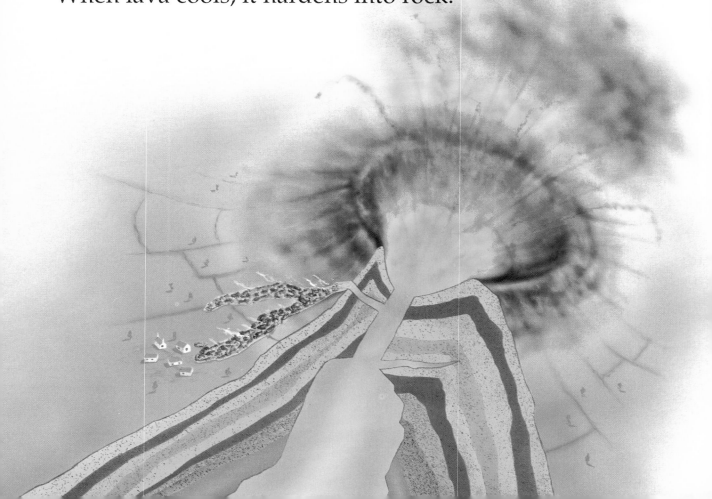

◁ This hill was once the inside of an old volcano. It is made of lava that cooled and hardened.

▽ When some volcanoes erupt the red-hot lava travels fast. It burns everything in its path.

7

What Is Fire?

Fire is the heat and light we feel and see when something burns. Fires often have flames. They usually need the **gas** called **oxygen** in order to burn. Air contains oxygen. This is why fanning or blowing on a fire makes it burn faster. Most things will burn. Some burn at a lower **temperature** than others.

▷ Many farmers burn off the stubbly remains after the harvest. They need to be careful. Fire spreads easily out in the open. This is because air contains oxygen.

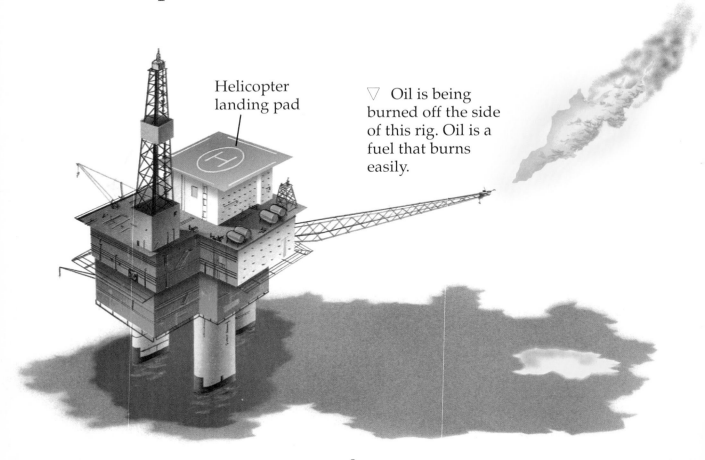

Helicopter landing pad

▽ Oil is being burned off the side of this rig. Oil is a fuel that burns easily.

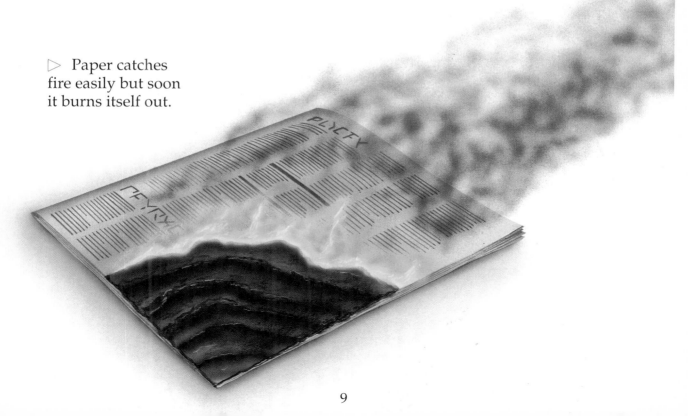

▷ Paper catches
fire easily but soon
it burns itself out.

Making Fire

Long ago, people discovered ways to make fire. Rubbing two materials together makes them heat up. If they heat up enough, some of them will catch fire. Also, striking a stone or a piece of metal with another hard material makes a spark. A spark may start a fire if it falls onto something that burns easily, like dry grass.

▽ This blacksmith is wearing goggles to protect his eyes from the sparks that fly up as he grinds an iron bar.

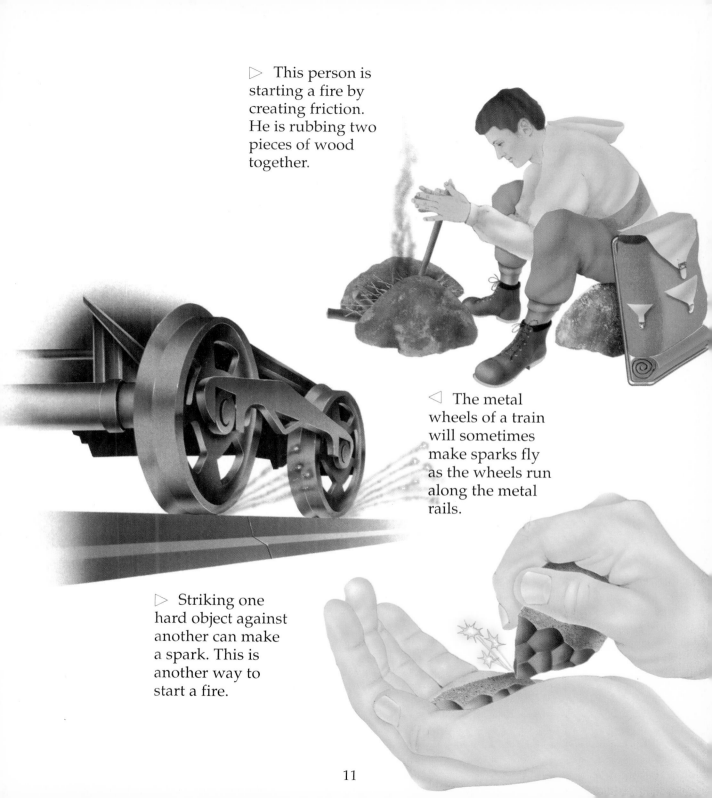

▷ This person is starting a fire by creating friction. He is rubbing two pieces of wood together.

◁ The metal wheels of a train will sometimes make sparks fly as the wheels run along the metal rails.

▷ Striking one hard object against another can make a spark. This is another way to start a fire.

11

Fire for Warmth and Light

In many parts of the world, people burn open fires to keep warm. They put wood or coal on the fire to keep it burning. Modern heating systems burn gas or oil. The flame is used to heat water or air.

Light is given off by very hot objects. A burning candle or a wire inside a bulb is hot.

▽ Wood burns well and is easily found. Open fires that burn wood keep people warm in many parts of the world.

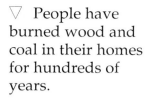

▽ People have burned wood and coal in their homes for hundreds of years.

◁▷ Simple lighting, such as a candle, uses a flame. The thin wire inside some bulbs glows when it is hot. It gives off a brighter light than a candle.

Fire for Cooking

Long ago, people learned how to cook their food with fire. Food can be cooked outside over an open flame. A lot of heat is lost in the open air. Simple stoves burn wood without losing that much heat. Modern gas stoves use a flame that you can control. Electric stoves have a metal tube over a coil of wire that gets very hot.

▷ Wood-burning stoves use less fuel than an open fire.

▽ You can cook food over a simple fire. You need to protect the food from the flames, or it will burn before it cooks.

▽ Modern stoves are easy to control. They waste very little heat.

Fire in Industry

Fire is used in **industry** to change materials. It can heat a metal and make it easier to bend. Fire can also heat a metal until it melts into a liquid. The liquid metal can then be molded into a new shape. Bricks are blocks of wet clay that have been "cooked". The heat dries them out and makes them hard. Plates and cups are made in the same way.

▷ In a hot furnace, metal will melt into a liquid.

▷ Pots, plates, and bricks made of clay can all be heated in a kiln to make them hard.

▷ The materials for making glass are first heated. The glass can then be shaped. This man is blowing glass.

Energy from Fire

Coal, gas, oil, and wood are all kinds of **fuel**. We burn fuel to release energy. This energy can then be used in many ways. Cars, trucks, planes, trains, and ships all burn fuel to make them move. We also burn fuel in some power plants. This makes heat, which boils water to make steam. The steam drives machinery that makes **electrical energy**.

▷ Jet engines burn large amounts of fuel. This gives the plane the energy and power needed for takeoff.

▽ Most vehicles burn gasoline in their engines. Gasoline is made from oil.

▽ Trains can be driven by steam. The energy comes from the fuel burning in the engine.

▷ Many power
plants burn coal
to make electrical
energy.

19

Forest Fires

Every summer, huge areas of forest are destroyed by fire. Many of the fires are started by people who camp and cook in the forest. The grass and wood is very dry. The smallest spark may make it burn. Forest fires can also be started by lightning. A flash of lightning is a huge spark of electrical energy. If it strikes a tree, the tree will catch fire.

▷ Every year there are huge forest fires. These fires destroy thousands of plants and kill many animals.

▽ Visitors to the forest need to be very careful. A smoldering fire may set grass and brushwood on fire.

◁ A forest will grow back after a fire, but this will take many years.

Pollution by Fire

Burning fuel gives off smoke and gases. Some of these can be dangerous. When there is too much of these gases in the air, the air becomes polluted. Plants and animals suffer in **polluted** air. We can help to stop pollution by burning less fuel. People are finding new ways to get energy from the sun and the wind.

▷ All fires give off gases. Burning rubber gives off dangerous black smoke.

▽ Forest trees help to clean the air. In many parts of the world, forests are being burned down to make room for cattle to graze. We should save forests from being destroyed.

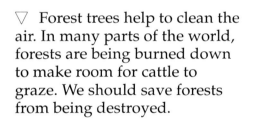

▽ This solar furnace gathers energy from the sun without causing air pollution.

Disasters with Fire

Terrible disasters can be caused by fire.
When volcanoes erupt, they release red
hot lava. The lava burns things in its path
as it flows downhill. Planes and cars
sometimes catch fire when they crash.
The fire is often made worse because of
the fuel in the vehicle. Buildings often
catch fire because of accidents with
heaters, stoves, or cigarettes.

▷ A fire will
spread if the
building contains
furniture and other
things that burn
easily.

▽ Planes carry
huge amounts of
fuel. In case of an
accident, the fuel
can cause very
serious fires.

Fire Fighting

Fire fighting is a highly skilled and dangerous job. People who fight fires are trained to know which part of the fire to attack first. They also know how to rescue people and prevent a fire from spreading. There are different kinds of equipment for different types of fires. Forest fires are sometimes put out by water sprayed from planes.

▷ Small aircraft are used to fight fires that spread over a large area.

▷ Every home should have a fire extinguisher for putting out small fires.

▷ Fire fighters carry hoses and other equipment on their fire engines. They connect the hoses to hydrants along the side of the street.

Fire and Safety

Fires can injure and kill people. They also destroy buildings and kill animals and plants. It is important to know how to prevent a fire. You also need to know what to do if a fire does start. Fire spreads when there is plenty of air. Closing doors and windows or covering a small fire with a blanket will help to keep it from spreading.

▷ A fire drill is a good way for people to practice what to do if there ever is a fire.

▽ Pressing the button on a fire alarm will set off a bell. This warns other people that a fire has started.

△ Every home should have a smoke alarm. This gives a very early warning of a fire.

▽ Most new furniture is made from materials that do not burn easily.

▷ The fire exits in public buildings are clearly marked.

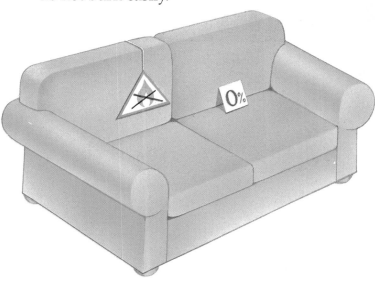

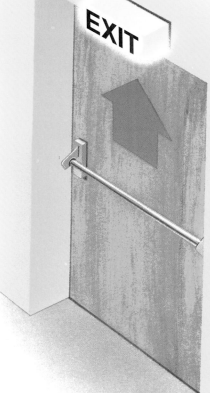

Things to Do

- Make a small collection of things that have been made or changed by heat. These could be glass, molded metal, pottery, cooked food, and so on.

- Make a fire escape plan for your home. Write down where the fire exits are. Think of a way to warn other people of a fire. Make sure you have a smoke detector and fire extinguisher.

- Make a collage on the theme of fire. You could include pictures of the sun, volcanoes, forest fires, and fire fighting.

Glossary

Centigrade   A scale used to measure how hot or cold something is. Water freezes at 0° C and boils at 100° C.

Crust   The hard outer surface that covers the Earth.

Electrical Energy   The flow of an electric current. Its energy is used to make light and heat, and to power a motor.

Energy   The ability to do work. When an object moves, it has energy. Heat and light are also forms of energy.

Fuel   A material like wood or coal that releases energy when it is burned.

Furnace   A place which can contain a fire. Furnaces are used to heat or melt things.

Gas   A substance that is not a solid or liquid. Air is a mixture of gases.

Industry   Work which is done in factories to make goods.

Lava   Molten rock that flows from a volcano.

Magma   Molten rock inside the Earth.

Molten   Metal or rock which is turned to liquid by very great heat.

Oxygen   A gas which nearly all living things need to survive.

Polluted   Spoiled by harmful substances.

Temperature   How hot or cold something is.

Transportation   Vehicles to move people or objects from one place to another.

Index

Photographic credits:
Austin J. Brown Aviation Picture Library 19; Bruce Coleman Limited 27; Eye Ubiquitous 23; Chris Fairclough Colour Library 10; Robert Harding Picture 3, 9, 15, 17, 21; Robinson/Oxford Scientific Films 5; Sefton Photo Library 25; Shout 29; Zefa Picture Library 7.